國家圖書館出版品預行編目資料

Tabitha Escapes from the Lions：小老鼠貝貝逃生記
／ Marc Ponomareff著；王平,倪靖,郜欣繪；本局編
輯部譯.－－初版一刷.－－臺北市：三民，2005
面；　　公分.－－(Fun心讀雙語叢書.小老鼠貝
貝歷險記系列)
中英對照
ISBN 957–14–4230–5　（精裝）
1. 英國語言－讀本
805.18　　　　　　　　　　　　　　94001180

網路書店位址　http://www.sanmin.com.tw

© **Tabitha Escapes from the Lions**
——小老鼠貝貝逃生記

著作人	Marc Ponomareff
繪　者	王 平　倪 靖　郜 欣
譯　者	本局編輯部
出版諮詢顧問	殷偉芳
發行人	劉振強
著作財產權人	三民書局股份有限公司 臺北市復興北路386號
發行所	三民書局股份有限公司 地址／臺北市復興北路386號 電話／(02)25006600 郵撥／0009998–5
印刷所	三民書局股份有限公司
門市部	復北店／臺北市復興北路386號 重南店／臺北市重慶南路一段61號
初版一刷	2005年2月
編　號	S 805131
定　價	新臺幣壹佰捌拾元整

行政院新聞局登記證局版臺業字第○二○○號

有著作權‧不准侵害

ISBN　957–14–4230–5　　（精裝）

For Justine

It had rained for many days in Africa. When the rain stopped, the elephants discovered a new water hole. It was deep, and perfect for taking baths in. But there was one problem — the lions had found it too, and they wanted it for themselves.

3

The animals began arguing*. The lions stood on one side of the water hole, roaring*, "The water hole is ours!"

The elephants stood on the other side, lifting their trunks* and trumpeting.

"This water hole belongs to everyone who lives here!" they trumpeted.

The leader of the lions noticed that a mouse was living with the elephants. The elephants seemed to be very fond of* this mouse. They even let her use their trunks as a water-slide. Soon the lion had thought of a plan that would cause* trouble for the elephants....

That night, Tabitha the mouse was sleeping beneath her tent of sticks*, near Jessica the elephant and her parents. A faint* sound woke her up. She saw two yellow-and-green eyes above her. They seemed to be glowing* in the dark.

Before she had a chance to call for help, a giant paw* covered her face!

The lion held Tabitha in his huge mouth, and locked her behind his long teeth, as he ran back to his den*. Then he spit* her out, as if she were a piece of chewing-gum — plop! — onto the ground.

Tabitha's fur* was all wet. Frowning*, she brushed herself off.
"Ugh!" she said. "This is really gross*."

She noticed, suddenly, that she was surrounded* by four lion cubs*. She kept very still*. The small lions stared at her, licking their lips.

"Do not EAT the prisoner*," their father warned* them. "And do not PLAY with the prisoner. As long as we keep this mouse alive, the elephants will do as we say. That new water hole will be ours."

Then he left the den, to go and tell the other lions how clever he was.

But Tabitha was not so easily kept a prisoner. She knew how much lion cubs liked to play.

She made her small body into a ball, and rolled herself beneath the cubs' noses. Sure enough, as soon as one cub began to move her across the ground with its paw, the others wanted to join in. They became more and more excited. Soon they piled on top of one another, growling*, and fell into a heap.

As the cubs tumbled* about, Tabitha rolled herself right out the door.

"It's been fun playing with you!" she laughed. "But I've got to be going now."

She ran as fast as she could back to the elephants' village, where she told Jessica and her parents what had happened....

The elephants laughed for a long time.

The next day, Tabitha was pleased to see the lions and
elephants sharing the water hole. The lions had decided that
sharing was a much easier thing to do than playing tricks on
elephants — or on mice!

生字表

adj.= 形容詞，n.= 名詞，v.= 動詞

故事中譯

p.2

非洲已經一連下了好幾天的雨。雨停了之後，大象們發現地上積了一個新的水坑。這個水坑很深，是個適合泡澡的好地方。但是有個問題出現了——那就是獅子們也發現了這個水坑，而且他們想要將這個水坑佔為己有。

p.4

他們雙方開始爭吵。獅子們站在水坑的一邊，吼著：「水坑是我們的！」

p.5

大象們站在另外一邊，高高舉起他們的象鼻子，發出像喇叭般的吼叫聲。

他們吼著說：「這個水坑屬於所有住在這裡的動物！」

p.6

這時，獅子的首領注意到

有隻老鼠跟大象們生活在一起，而且大象們似乎非常喜歡這隻老鼠，甚至讓她把他們的象鼻子當水上溜滑梯來玩。沒過多久，獅子頭目就想到了一個會帶給大象們麻煩的計畫……

p.8

那天晚上，小老鼠貝貝在象寶寶小潔跟她父母旁邊，一個用小木棍搭起的帳棚裡睡著。這個時候，一個微弱的聲音驚醒了她。她看到在她的上方有兩隻又黃又綠的眼睛，彷彿在黑暗中發亮著。在她有機會呼救之前，一個巨大的腳掌蓋住了她的臉！

p.10

在獅子一路奔回他的洞穴時，他把貝貝放在他的大嘴裡，關在長長的牙齒後面。到了之後，他把貝貝像口香糖一樣吐了出來，結果貝貝就啪噠一聲，摔在地上。

p.11

　　貝貝的毛全都濕透了。她皺著眉頭，把自己梳理乾淨，還一邊說：「噁！這真是有夠噁心的。」

p.12

　　突然間，她發現自己被四隻小獅子包圍著。她一動也不敢動。小獅子們盯著她看，還一邊舔著他們的嘴唇。

p.13

　　但是他們的父親警告他們：「別把咱們的俘虜給吃了，也不准跟她玩。只要我們留著這隻老鼠不殺，大象就會照著我們的話做。這樣，新的水坑就會是我們的了。」

　　然後他離開了洞穴，去告訴其他的獅子們，他有多聰明。

p.14

　　但是貝貝可沒那麼容易屈服，願意當他們的俘虜。她知道小獅子們很愛玩，於是她把自己小小的身體蜷成一顆球，然後滾到小獅子們的鼻子下面。可想而知，當其中一隻小獅子開始用腳掌把她滾到地板的另一邊時，其他的小獅子也想加入這個遊戲。他們變得越來越興奮。才一下子，他們就一隻疊在另一隻上面、咆哮著，最後摔成了一堆。

p.16

趁小獅子們在地上跌跌撞撞的時候，貝貝把自己滾出了門外。

她笑著說：「跟你們一起玩真的很有趣，但是現在我得走囉！」

p.17

她全速跑回大象的村落，然後告訴小潔跟她的父母所有事情發生的經過……

大象們笑了好久好久。

p.19

隔天，貝貝看到獅子和大象們

24

一起分享那個水坑時，非常
的開心。原來，獅子們已經決定，
共同分享水坑，要比對大象或對老鼠耍卑鄙
的手段，來得簡單的多了。

25

看ㄎㄢˋ 圖ㄊㄨˊ 學ㄒㄩㄝˊ 單ㄉㄢ 字ㄗˋ

小ㄒㄧㄠˇ 朋ㄆㄥˊ 友ㄧㄡˇ ， 在ㄗㄞˋ 玩ㄨㄢˊ 這ㄓㄜˋ 個ㄍㄜˋ 遊ㄧㄡˊ 戲ㄒㄧˋ 前ㄑㄧㄢˊ ， 請ㄑㄧㄥˇ 先ㄒㄧㄢ 按ㄢˋ 下ㄒㄧㄚˋ track 4 ， 聽ㄊㄧㄥ 一ㄧˋ 遍ㄅㄧㄢˋ 下ㄒㄧㄚˋ 面ㄇㄧㄢˋ 的ㄉㄜ˙ 單ㄉㄢ 字ㄗˋ ， 並ㄅㄧㄥˋ 試ㄕˋ 試ㄕˋ 看ㄎㄢˋ 跟ㄍㄣ 著ㄓㄜ˙ 一ㄧˋ 起ㄑㄧˇ 念ㄋㄧㄢˋ 。 單ㄉㄢ 字ㄗˋ 念ㄋㄧㄢˋ 熟ㄕㄡˊ 了ㄌㄜ˙ 以ㄧˇ 後ㄏㄡˋ ， 再ㄗㄞˋ 按ㄢˋ 下ㄒㄧㄚˋ track 5 ， 你ㄋㄧˇ 會ㄏㄨㄟˋ 聽ㄊㄧㄥ 到ㄉㄠˋ 下ㄒㄧㄚˋ 面ㄇㄧㄢˋ 故ㄍㄨˋ 事ㄕˋ 中ㄓㄨㄥ 文ㄨㄣˊ 的ㄉㄜ˙ 部ㄅㄨˋ 分ㄈㄣˋ ； 遇ㄩˋ 到ㄉㄠˋ 有ㄧㄡˇ 圖ㄊㄨˊ 的ㄉㄜ˙ 地ㄉㄧˋ 方ㄈㄤ ， 就ㄐㄧㄡˋ 要ㄧㄠˋ 由ㄧㄡˊ 你ㄋㄧˇ 把ㄅㄚˇ 圖ㄊㄨˊ 片ㄆㄧㄢˋ 代ㄉㄞˋ 表ㄅㄧㄠˇ 的ㄉㄜ˙ 英ㄧㄥ 文ㄨㄣˊ 單ㄉㄢ 字ㄗˋ 大ㄉㄚˋ 聲ㄕㄥ 的ㄉㄜ˙ 喊ㄏㄢˇ 出ㄔㄨ 來ㄌㄞˊ ， 看ㄎㄢˋ 看ㄎㄢˋ 你ㄋㄧˇ 都ㄉㄡ 會ㄏㄨㄟˋ 了ㄌㄜ˙ 嗎ㄇㄚ˙ ？

 paw

 den

 Fur

 cub

獅子們和大象們都想要把水坑佔為己有，於是獅子爸爸就用他的，抓走了大象的好朋友，小老鼠貝貝。獅子爸爸回到他的，「呸！」的一聲把貝貝從嘴裡吐出來；貝貝的都濕了，覺得自己黏答答的好噁心。這時候，愛玩的搶著要跟貝貝玩遊戲，貝貝想到一個可以脫身的方法：她讓用他們的，把貝貝當成球一樣在地上滾。等到越玩越興奮的在地上摔成一團，貝貝就趁機逃出啦！

　　最後，請小朋友們按下 track 6，再把這個故事念一遍。

一次可怕的經驗——
關於獅子的小知識

大家好，我是小老鼠貝貝。你們一定知道，我曾經因為獅子跟大象爭水池的問題，被獅子抓去了吧！那真是一次可怕的經驗。

我在黑夜裡被獅子爸爸抓到一個陌生的地方，那不是森林，而是一大片草原，黑暗中隱約有看到幾顆樹。那裡有很多其他的獅子，有公有母，還有小獅子，讓我想起以前聽人家說過，**獅子是以一個或幾個家族為單位，群居在一起，多的時候還會有四十隻**呢。我在地上發現很多骨頭，應該是那些淪為獅子食物的動物吧！可憐的**鹿、斑馬和羚羊**，應該是在驚恐中受到**負責獵食的母獅**的攻擊吧！

獅子爸爸把我從他嘴裡吐出來，這時我才清楚看見他的模樣：他**四腳著地時，高度超過一公尺，**

從頭到尾巴大概有三公尺這麼長；他的頭部最明顯的是有一圈鬃毛圍在臉部外面，一直延伸到肩膀甚至胸前。金色和棕色的鬃毛看起來鬆鬆軟軟的，還摻雜一些黑色；我想，這圈鬃毛最大的好處，是可以讓獅子輕易躲在顏色相近的枯草裡，而不被發現吧。

跟在獅子爸爸後面的是幾隻小獅子，看起來活力充沛。他們一看到我就變得很興奮，一隻隻朝我撲過來；我雖然很害怕，卻也看清楚他們的長相：臉部沒有明顯的一圈鬃毛，但是有明顯的斑點；這時我才確定他們是剛出生不久的小獅子。我知道小獅子們愛玩，所以陪他們在地上滾了一陣子，最後等他們精疲力盡了，我才匆匆忙忙的逃出來。

現在你們知道，我在那天晚上經歷的事情了吧！雖然那是一次很驚險的經驗，不過也讓我更了解獅子們。還好爭水池的事情，最後以和平的方式解決了，要不然，這場爭執不知道要到什麼時候才會結束呢！